First American Edition

Library of Congress Catalog Card Number 86-47830
ISBN 0-316-04260-9

First published in Great Britain
by Methuen Children's Books Ltd.

Printed in Hong Kong

Truffles in Trouble

CATHERINE ANHOLT

Joy Street Books

Boston · Little, Brown and Company · Toronto

"Wake up, Truffles!" Mother called. "It's time for breakfast."

Truffles hurried to the table. He reached for the teapot.
Crash!
"Run off and play like a good little pig," Father said.
"I'd like some peace and quiet."

Truffles decided to practice his hammering.

Next he played his drum.

He sailed his boats. Then he went for a ride on his bicycle.

Truffles was very pleased with himself.
He knew how to be a good little pig.

Mother was not pleased at all. She gave him a long list of things
to get at the store. "This should keep you out of trouble," she said.

"Butter, eggs, milk," Truffles repeated. "Tea, sugar, carrots."

But when he got to the bridge, he stopped to sail his boats.

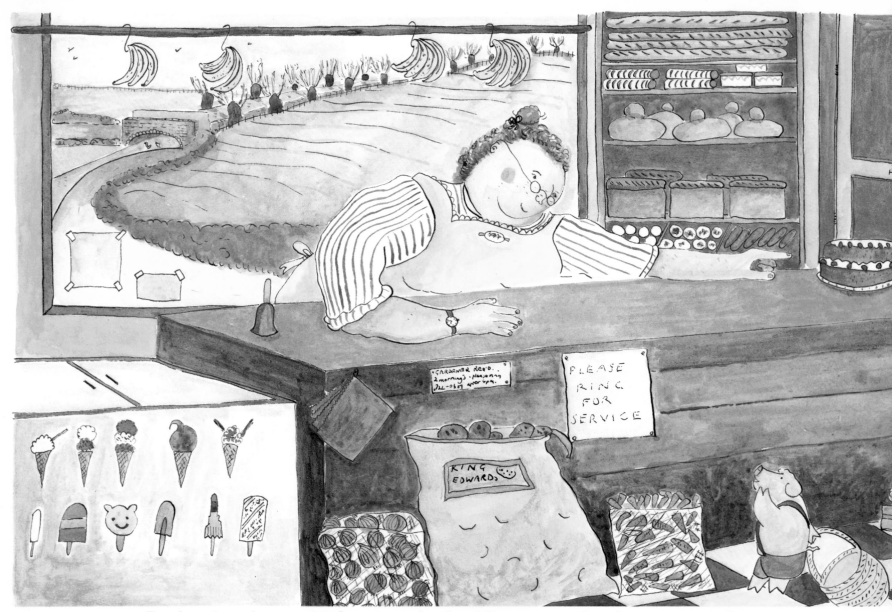

By the time he got to the store, he had forgotten what he was sent for.
Where was his list?

"Let's see," said Mrs. Brown. "Was it cake?"
"Oh yes!" said Truffles. "Lots of cakes!"

When he got home, Truffles laid the cakes out on the table.
"Look what I got," he said proudly.
"Truffles, what have you done?" Mother cried. "Didn't you look at my list?"

Truffles knew he was in trouble now.
Being a good little pig wasn't easy — but suddenly he had an idea.

First he vacuumed the living room.

He picked up his toys.

He cleaned up the bathroom,

and worked in the garden.
He didn't break a thing!

When Father came home, Truffles ran to meet him.
"How's my favorite little pig?" said Father.

"There's nothing like some peace and quiet," said Father after dinner.
"Has Truffles been this good all day?"
"Yes," said Mother, "all day," and she winked. But Truffles was already fast asleep.